The ~~VERY~~ NOISY FOXES

By
Amy HUSBAND

TOP™
THAT

Licensed exclusively to Top That Publishing Ltd
Tide Mill Way, Woodbridge, Suffolk, IP12 1AP, UK
www.topthatpublishing.com
Copyright © 2014 Amy Husband
All rights reserved
4 6 8 9 7 5 3
Manufactured in Bulgaria

Written and illustrated by Amy Husband

ISBN 978-1-78445-227-8

A catalogue record for this book is available from the British Library

'For Dad, who inspired this story'

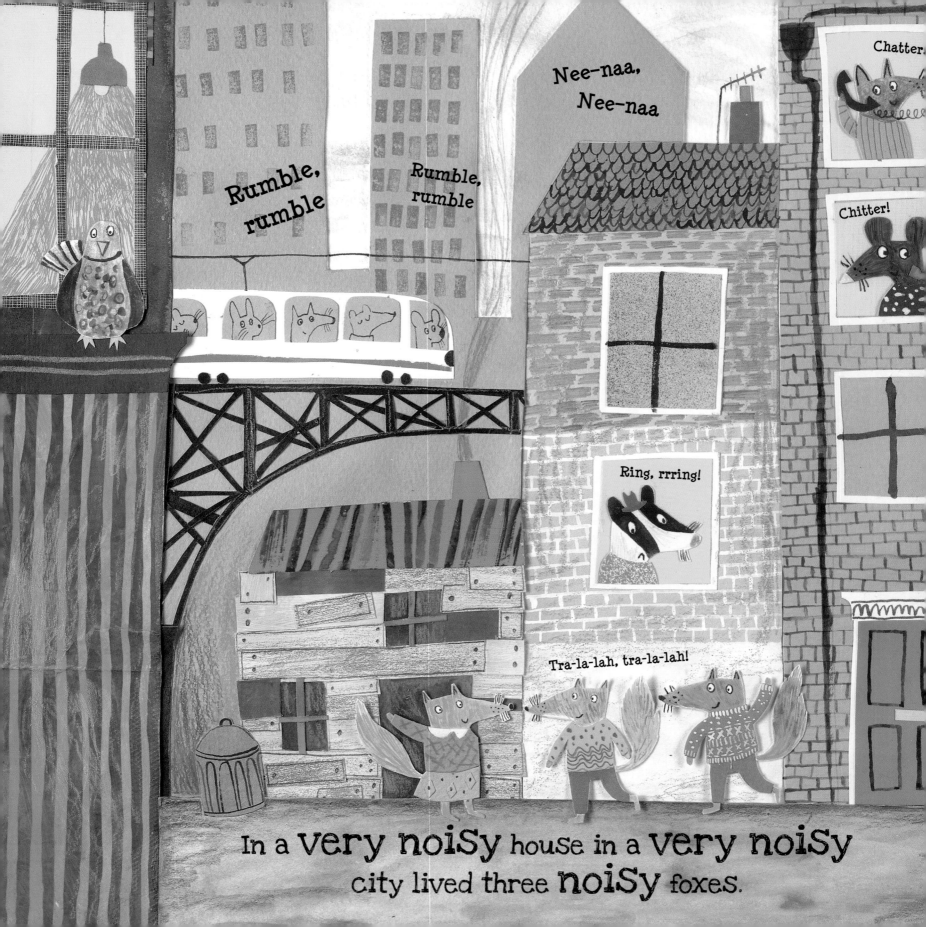

In a **very noisy** house in a **very noisy** city lived three **noisy** foxes.

'Wouldn't it be nice to be quiet sometimes?' asked Fox Number One.

'Perhaps we should move to the countryside,' suggested Fox Number Two.

'What a good idea!' replied Fox Number Three.

HONK-
HOOONK!

VVRRROOOOOOMMMM!

So they packed up all of their **very noisy** things,
and caught the **very noisy** bus, to find a place
to live in the very quiet **countryside**.

TOOT-
TOOT-
TOOOOT!

BEEP!

BEEP!
BEEP!

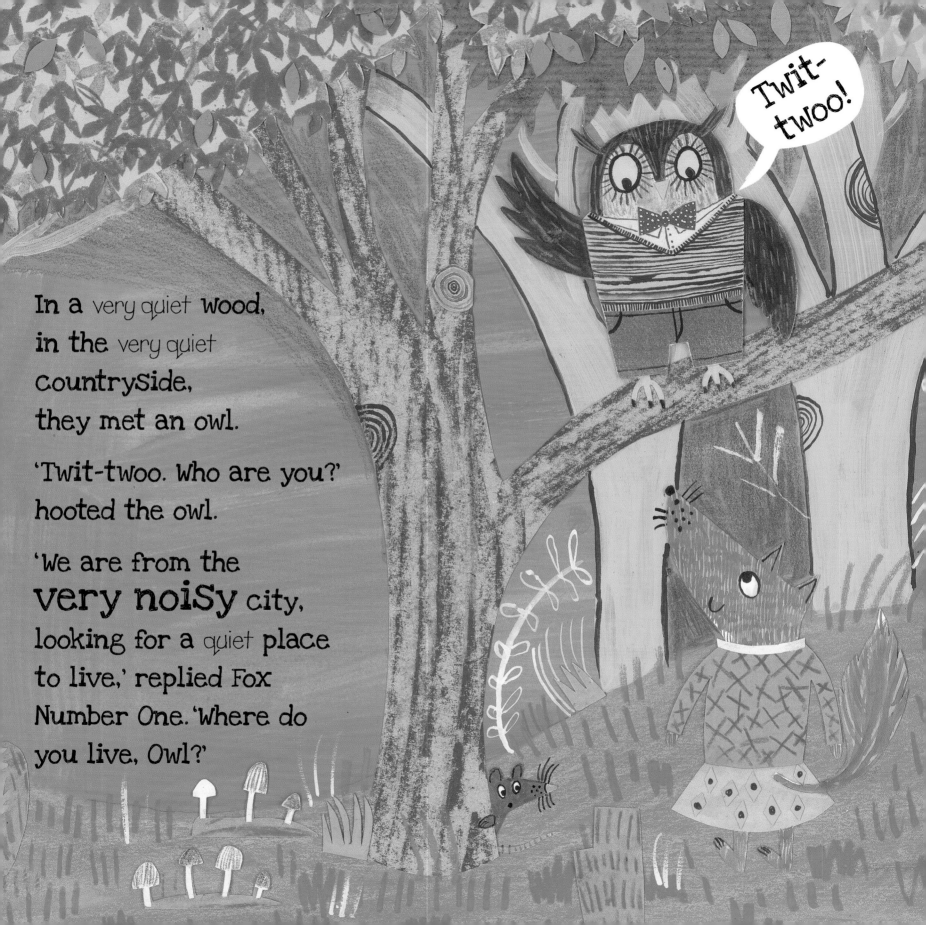

Twit-twoo!

In a very quiet **wood**,
in the very quiet
countryside,
they met an owl.

'Twit-twoo. Who are you?'
hooted the owl.

'We are from the
very noiSy city,
looking for a quiet place
to live,' replied Fox
Number One. 'Where do
you live, Owl?'

'I live up here at the top of this very tall, quiet tree,' the owl said.

'Oh yes, it is very quiet, but it is too high for us,' said Fox Number One. 'We're scared!'

Next, in a very quiet meadow, in the very quiet countryside the noisy foxes met a mole, who popped up out of the ground.

'Hello, Mole. We are from the noisy city looking for a quiet place to live. Can you help us?' asked Fox Number Two.

'Oh yes, I live in a very quiet place,'
replied the mole. 'Follow me
and I'll show you.'

In a very quiet clearing in the very quiet countryside, the **noisy** foxes met a frog.

'Ribbit, ribbit. What do you three **noisy** foxes want?' the frog asked.

'We are looking for a quiet place to live,' said Fox Number Three. 'Where do you live, Frog?'

'Come with me and I'll show you,' replied the frog.

'I live here in this very quiet pond,' said the frog.

'Oh yes, it is very quiet indeed, but it is too wet for us,' said Fox Number Three. 'And we can't swim!'

So the three noisy foxes kept searching for a very, very long time and they ended up in the very quietest part of the countryside, a long, long way from the very noisy city. As they ventured along the very quiet path, they met a badger.

'Hello, Badger. We are looking for a quiet place to live,' said the noisy foxes. 'Can you help us? We have looked everywhere.'

'Yes, of course. Follow me,' replied the badger.

'This is where I live,' said the badger.
'It is the quietest place in all of the countryside.'

'Oh yes, it really is very quiet, and very lovely.
It might just be the perfect place,' said the
noisy foxes. 'But ...

... it is just TOO quiet!'

The **noisy** foxes were
really fed up with being *quiet!*
So they started to make some noise.
As they banged and clanged and
chittered and chattered, a *quiet* little mouse scurried up to them.

'What is all this noise about?' asked the *quiet* little mouse.

'We need a place to live, but it can't be too high, it can't be too dark,
it can't be too wet, and it definitely can't be *too quiet.*'

'I know the perfect place,' squeaked the mouse. 'Follow me.'

'Well done, little mouse. This really is the perfect place!'